"Come on!" Luke urged us from above.

Finally, I made it up to the rocks where Luke was crouched over the dark hole in the ground.

"Here you go." I handed him the clothes hose.

Luke looked it over and tugged at a few of the knots. "Good. Great. Good work."

He leaned back toward the hole. "Amber?"

"Yes?" Her voice sounded weak and distant.

"I'm going to send down a line," Luke said. "Yell when it gets to you." Luke started to feed the clothes hose into the hole, but it wasn't long before he stopped.

"What's wrong?" I asked.

"It's not going down," he said. "It's bunching somewhere before it gets to Amber."

"So what can you do?" I asked.

Luke stared at me in the dark for a moment. "Someone's going to have to go down and bring the line to her."

Books by Todd Strasser

AGAINST THE ODDS™: Shark Bite
AGAINST THE ODDS™: Grizzly Attack
AGAINST THE ODDS™: Buzzard's Feast

From Minstrel Books
Published by POCKET BOOKS

TODD STRASSER

AGAINST THE ODDS™

BUZZARD'S FEAST

A
MINSTREL®
BOOK

Published by POCKET BOOKS
New York London Toronto Sydney Tokyo Singapore

A MINSTREL PAPERBACK *Original*

A Minstrel Book published by
POCKET BOOKS, a division of Simon & Schuster Inc.
1230 Avenue of the Americas, New York, NY 10020

™ and Copyright © 1999 by Todd Strasser

ISBN: 0-671-02311-X

First Minstrel Books printing January 1999

10 9 8 7 6 5 4 3 2 1

A MINSTREL BOOK and colophon are registered trademarks of Simon & Schuster Inc.

Front cover illustration by Franco Accornero

Printed in the U.S.A.

To Rose Emma Birnbaum and Zoe Danielle Birnbaum

BUZZARD'S FEAST

1

"You sure about this, Henry?" my nine-year-old brother Paul asked me. We were standing across the street from a small white house in Pasadena, which is a suburb of Los Angeles. Parked on the street in front of the house was a dented brown van with a metal ladder and a big green metal can on the back. It was in that van that I hoped my brother and I would make the 200-mile trip across the desert to visit our dad in Las Vegas.

"Pretty sure," I answered. But the truth was that I wasn't certain. Mostly, I was nervous because we weren't doing what our mom wanted us to do, which was take the bus to Las Vegas. Mom had recently put her mom (our grandmother) in a nursing home, and it was costing her a ton of money. She'd given us money for the bus, but I knew she really couldn't afford it, so after she went to work that morning, I put the money in an envelope with a note saying Paul and I were getting a ride to Las Vegas instead. I left the note on the kitchen counter where she was sure to see it.

Across the street, the door to the small white house opened and Amber came out. Amber was a girl I knew from school. She had short brown hair, an impish smile, and lively eyes. I really didn't know her very well, but I liked her because she always seemed to be in a good mood. Her brother Luke owned the van.

"Hey, guys!" Amber waved and smiled. Paul and I picked up our backpacks and crossed the street.

"Looks like you're ready to go," Amber said.

"Yeah," I said. "This is my brother, Paul."

Paul and Amber shook hands.

"So," I said, "are you ready?"

"Soon," Amber answered. "Luke's still trying to get his act together."

"What does that mean?" Paul asked.

"Nothing, really," Amber answered with a shrug. "He's just not the most organized person in the world, but he'll be ready in a little while.

Besides, he says we're better off crossing the desert at night. It's not as hot then."

"So he's done this before?" I asked.

"Cross the desert?" Amber replied. "Oh, sure, plenty of times. He and his friends like to go out into the desert and just hang out. I don't know what's so great about it, but Luke says it's really cool."

Just then the front door of the house opened and a big, heavyset guy with long blond dreadlocks came out. His skin was darkly tanned and you could see that he spent a lot of time outside. He was wearing lots of leather-and-rope halyards around his neck and wrists. His T-shirt was tie-dyed bright green, blue, and yellow, and he was wearing khaki commando shorts with lots of big pockets.

"Hey, dudes!" He smiled and ambled down toward us.

Amber introduced us.

"So, you guys ready for a big adventure?" Luke asked.

"We just want to go to see our dad in Las Vegas," answered Paul. Because he was nine, he tended to take things pretty literally. He and I were already nervous enough about disobeying our mom and taking this ride instead of the bus.

3

"Yeah." Luke nodded. "That's what I meant, little dude."

"It's going to be okay, right?" Paul asked, pointing at the banged-up van parked at the curb. "I mean, your van'll make it?"

"Bertha?" Luke grinned. "Don't worry, little dude—she's never failed me yet."

2

One of the reasons Luke wasn't quite ready to go was that Bertha was full of gardening equipment. It turned out that the reason Luke was so tanned was that he cut people's lawns for a living. So before we could start our journey, we had to help him get the lawnmowers, grass blowers, rakes, and other stuff out of the back of the van and into the garage.

"Great," Luke said when we'd finished. He was dusting his hands off in the shade of the garage. "Now we just have to make you guys comfortable."

I didn't understand what he meant until he asked us to help him drag an old mattress out of the garage and down to the curb, where we put it in the back of the van.

5

Now I understood. The only seats in the van were for the driver and the passenger beside him. The other passengers had to ride on the mattress in the back. There were two windows in the back doors and none along the sides.

While Luke went back into the house to get some stuff, Paul and I looked around the inside of the van. Inside, you could see how old Bertha really was. The dashboard was sun-bleached and cracked and the sun visors were missing.

The cushioning on the seats was splitting and you could see the old yellow foam rubber underneath. In some places, the seats were so cracked that they were patched with silver duct tape.

"Don't worry, guys," Amber said. "I know it looks kind of junky, but my brother really loves this van. He takes great care of her."

"Make yourselves comfortable," Luke said, coming out of the house. He threw some old, seedy-looking blankets in the back. Also back there was a greasy cardboard box filled with quarts of oil in silver plastic bottles, and some old green garden hose. The back of the van smelled of gasoline, oil, and dried grass.

Paul and I crawled in, dragging our backpacks with us. We sat down on the old mattress. Luke and Amber got in the front.

"Uh, what about seat belts?" Paul asked, since our mom always made us wear them.

6

"Don't worry about it, little dude," Luke said as he slid the key into the ignition.

"But isn't it against the law not to wear them?" Paul asked.

"Not for us," Luke replied. "As long as we're in this van, we're grandfathered."

Paul turned and gave me a silent frown to show he didn't know what that meant. Neither did I, but I was distracted by the sound of Luke starting the van.

Or, I guess I should say, *trying* to start the van.

When Luke turned the key, the engine made a lot of whining, groaning sounds, but it didn't start. In the front seat, Luke let go of the key. In the silence that followed, I seriously began to wonder if Paul and I were making a mistake.

But then Luke turned the key again. This time the engine groaned once, then churned and grumbled to life. The next thing I knew, we pulled away from the curb. Like it or not, we were on our way.

3

Paul and I sat on the mattress, using our backpacks as cushions against the bare metal walls of the van. It was hot inside Bertha. I could feel the heat coming in through the windows as the van wound through the streets and toward the expressway.

"Do you have any air-conditioning?" I asked.

"Doesn't work," Luke replied as he fiddled with a portable CD player on the floor between his seat and Amber's. Suddenly, loud, thumping music began to blast out of speakers in the back. The air-conditioning might not have worked, but the sound system was state of the art.

I was beginning to see that we weren't going to enjoy the ride. We were only a few minutes into the trip and it was already pretty uncomfortable. The van seemed to find every bump in the road and magnify it, especially in the back where Paul and I were. A couple of times, Paul and I actually bounced into the air. Each time that happened, my brother and I would share a dismal look as we adjusted our backpacks and leaned against them again.

"So, your old man lives in Vegas, huh?" Luke called over the music. "What's he do?"

"He's a blackjack dealer at the Mirage," Paul answered.

"What do you do while he's working?" Amber asked.

"He's got a pool at his house," I said. "We hang out there mostly."

I guess talking would have been one way to make the trip go faster, but the music was so loud it was hard to have much of a conversation. Paul and I spent most of our time craning our necks to catch glimpses through the windshield and the windows in the front doors.

The highway took us out of the suburbs. We watched as the tightly packed white houses, green lawns, and blue pools gave way to trailer parks and junkyards. Soon we were passing farmlands kept green by irrigation.

Then we entered what felt like another world—the desert. The green lawns were replaced by barren yellow-brown sand and brown-gray rock. Here and there, the earth was dotted with patches of grayish creosote bushes and gray-green cactus. We found ourselves gazing at mile after mile of dry expanse peppered with stringy plants, boulders bleached by the sun, dried-out ravines, and dusty-looking mountains looming in the background.

All around us, the distance was blurred by waves of heat rising and drifting lazily over the ground. Despite the open windows in the front and the steady breeze blowing in, the back of the van felt uncomfortably hot. The heat and steady droning of Bertha's engine started to make me feel drowsy.

"Hey! What's that?" Paul leaned forward and pointed through the windshield. In the distance ahead of us was a huge statue of a horse rearing up on its hind legs. Behind it were some buildings.

"Just the Roy Rogers Museum," Luke answered in a tone that indicated he had no interest in stopping.

Paul slid back. He pursed his lips and stared at the van's floor, disappointed.

But a few miles past the museum, Luke pulled the van off the road for no apparent reason. We watched as he got out, opened the van's hood, then checked something. The next thing I knew, he came around to the back of the van and pulled open the back doors. Paul and I

10

squinted out into the bright sunlight as Luke rummaged through the plastic quart bottles of oil and found a few that were full.

"What's wrong?" Paul asked.

"She leaks oil," Luke answered. "I have to throw a couple of quarts in every hundred miles."

"You have enough to get us to Las Vegas?" I asked, forcing a smile on my face so it seemed like I was just joking around.

"Not yet," Luke answered, "but I will after we stop at The Last Place on Earth."

4

Bang! Luke slammed Bertha's doors closed, sending Paul and me back into the shadows.

Paul gave me a funny look. "What's The Last Place on Earth?"

"You've got me," I answered with a shrug and turned to Amber in the passenger seat. "Any ideas?"

"I think it's a store or something," Amber said. "Luke's always talking about what a cool place it is."

A few minutes later, Luke finished putting oil in the motor. He slammed down the hood and got back into the van.

Paul immediately asked him about The Last Place on Earth.

"It's this general store on the edge of the desert," Luke explained as he started Bertha and pulled the van back onto the highway. "You'll get a kick out of it."

We started down the highway again. Paul and I settled against our backpacks, but the surroundings were so desolate and the van so rickety that I couldn't help wondering what would happen if the van broke down. I tried not to think about it, but no matter what I did, the question wouldn't go away.

Finally, I slid forward to the space between Luke's and Amber's seats. The music was so loud, Luke didn't even notice me for a few moments.

"Hey, what's up?" he asked when he finally saw me.

"I was just wondering," I replied. "What happens if we break down in the desert?"

"No problem," Luke answered confidently. "We've got an eight-gallon water can, blankets, a flashlight, and all kinds of other stuff."

I nodded. That sounded reassuring.

"Besides," Luke went on, "I've spent a lot of time in the desert. Once you get to know her, you realize there's really not that much to be afraid of. I could probably survive out here for a long time even without water and supplies."

I slid back and rejoined my brother, feeling better. Luke sounded like he knew what he was talking about.

5

A little while later, we felt the van begin to slow down. Looking out through the windshield, I saw a ramshackle store up ahead with a big hand-painted sign above it that said:

THE LAST PLACE ON EARTH
Last Gas
Last Food and Water
Abandon All Hope Ye Who Pass And Don't Shop

"What's that last thing mean?" Paul asked me.

"I think it's a joke," I answered. That wasn't the only joke. As we got closer, I began to see that The Last Place on Earth looked like a joke, too. It was an old wooden barnlike place with all kinds of knickknacks hanging outside. One outside wall appeared to be covered with old license plates rusting and fading in the sun. There were a couple of brightly painted totem poles standing in the dirt, and in the back, we could see the hulks of rusting cars and a tall plume of black smoke from a fire. In the still desert air, the smoke rose straight up into the sky.

"You're gonna love this place," Luke said as he slowed down and stopped the van next to an ancient-looking red gasoline pump. Like everything else around The Last Place on Earth, it was sun-bleached and rusty.

Luke and Amber got out of Bertha and headed inside. Paul and I gave each other a look, then followed. As we pushed through the screen door of the store, a bell rang and the dusty, worn floorboards squeaked. Paul and I stopped and looked around. Luke was right. This was about the strangest store we'd ever been in.

Like most gasoline–convenience stores, it had a few aisles of shelves stocked with cans of soup, boxes of cereal, and chips and dips. And it had some big glass coolers covered with a film of condensation and filled with soft drinks. But that was where any similarity to any other store ended. Lining the walls above the shelves was the strangest assortment of stuffed animals and reptiles I'd ever seen.

It was like a museum. Amber and I walked along in awe, staring up at brown rattlesnakes with their fangs bared and at black-and-gold Gila monsters. There were cute gray-brown prairie dogs standing on their hind legs. There were coyotes, hawks, and big jackrabbits that were almost the size of small dogs. A large, fearsome-looking vulture with an ugly red head and a pointy-hooked beak glared down at us.

" 'Turkey vulture,' " Amber read from a small plaque. "Does that mean it's a turkey or a vulture?"

"My dad calls them buzzards," I answered.

"Henry!" Paul called from the back of the store. "Check this out!"

Amber and I went down an aisle and joined him beside a dusty glass case. Inside was a vast collection of dead scorpions, some as big as crayfish, others so small they could fit on a quarter.

"Oh, gross!" Amber grunted. "Sorry, guys, this is where I get off. See you outside."

She turned and quickly walked away, but Paul and I stayed at the display case, staring at the collection of creatures preserved under the glass.

"The darker and smaller they are, the more deadly," a deep voice said behind us.

Paul and I spun around. Standing behind us was a tall, thin man with long gray hair that was held back by a leather band around his forehead. He had a bushy gray beard and was wearing a blue Western shirt. His neck and wrists were covered with silver-and-turquoise jewelry.

"Come over here, boys," he said. "I want to show you something I think you'll like."

He walked with a limp. The heel of his left cowboy boot was worn down at an odd angle that made him walk bowlegged. He led us to a counter at the front of the store and went behind it. By now, I'd figured out that he either owned the store or at least worked there. While Paul and I stared at the old brass cash register on the counter, the gray-haired man reached under the counter.

"Ah!" Paul yelped and jumped back as the man placed the biggest spider I'd ever seen on the counter. It was brown and covered with fur-like hair. I recognized immediately that it was a tarantula, but I had never seen one close up, and I was pretty certain Paul hadn't either.

Left alone on the counter, the big spider cautiously felt its way around as if it was uncertain where it was. Paul and I watched, fascinated.

"Go ahead, pick him up," the man said. "He won't hurt."

My brother and I shared a look. Neither of us

17

was going to touch that thing, no matter what this guy said. The man behind the counter grinned and scooped the tarantula up into his hands. Paul and I watched in amazement as he placed the big spider on the front of his shirt and left him there.

"See? He's as tame as a dog," the old man said. "I got a tamed scorpion back here, too. Want to see it?"

Paul and I shook our heads.

"So . . . you boys comin' or goin'?" the man asked.

Paul scowled. Neither of us knew what he meant.

"The desert," the man explained as he gently stroked the tarantula's fuzzy back with his finger. "You comin' out or goin' in?"

"Going through," Paul corrected him.

"Got yourselves enough water?" the man asked.

Paul and I nodded.

"That's good," the man said with a grin. "You don't want to run out of water out there. It ain't no fun to die of thirst."

"We're not walking," Paul stressed. "We're driving."

"Don't make no difference," the man replied with a shrug. "Desert's as tough on vehicles as it is on humans. The sand and heat just grinds you down."

"Is that why you have all those old cars outside?" Paul asked.

The man nodded. "You can keep them going for a while, but sooner or later the sand just gets into everything, and then they seize up and freeze and even the junk man don't want 'em."

Luke came up beside us and slid a big cardboard box full of plastic motor oil bottles on the counter. "Nice spider," he said to the man as naturally as if he were complimenting someone on his tie.

"Thanks." The man behind the counter nodded down at the case of motor oil. "Anything else?"

Luke looked over at Paul and me. "You guys want to pick up anything cold to drink, this is your last chance."

Paul and I both went over to the soda displays and got large bottles of pop and brought them back to the counter.

"Might want to take a few spares," the man behind the counter suggested.

But Luke shook his head. "They won't need it," he said.

The man behind the counter nodded ominously. "Lot of people say that," he said. "It's funny how many of them are wrong."

6

Clutching our cold bottles of pop, we followed Luke out of the store. At the doorway, Paul paused to pick through a cardboard box filled with free literature. He was funny that way. He was always incredibly curious about things and didn't mind reading the way I did. He'd read just about anything.

Amber was waiting for us in Bertha. She was drinking a soda. Droplets of perspiration covered her forehead. Luke carried the case of oil back to the van and put it inside, but instead of getting in himself, he went around the side of the store.

"Where's he going?" I asked Amber, but she just shrugged.

Out of curiosity, Paul and I followed Luke. We

found him standing in the hot sun behind the store, not far from the big fire that was sending the black smoke high into the air.

As Paul and I caught up to him, we could feel the heat of the fire on our faces. It was a weird sensation, standing in the hot sun with this additional heat. Weirder still was how close Luke stood to the fire—so close that our faces almost felt like they were burning and the heat was almost unbearable. We could see now that it was a pile of old car tires burning. The acrid black smoke had a nasty chemical smell.

Paul and I could stand there for only a moment before we both had to back away. The heat of the fire, combined with the heat of the sun, was too much for us.

We backed away and stood in the shade of the store. I don't know why we didn't go back to the van. There was something about the way Luke just stood there staring at the fire that must have fascinated us, I guess. It was as if he loved the heat.

Finally, he turned and came back toward us. Even though he was really tan, we could see how the skin on his face and arms had been reddened by standing so close to the fire.

"How come you did that?" Paul asked him.

"Just wanted to see how long I could stand it," Luke answered mysteriously.

I can't say his answer made a lot of sense to me, but maybe it didn't matter. We got back into the van again and, with Luke driving, headed away from The Last Place on Earth and into the desert. In the back of the van, Paul opened one of the free pamphlets he'd gotten in the store. The title was "Desert Survival." As soon as he started to read, I knew there'd be no talking to him. That was just the way Paul was when he got involved in reading. It was like the rest of the world ceased to exist.

Instead, I slid up toward the front and into the space between Amber and her brother. When I got close to Luke, my nose filled again with the scent of that acrid smoke from the tire fire.

"This is gonna work out fine, just fine," Luke was saying. "In another couple of hours, the sun'll be down and it'll cool off and we'll have a nice ride through the desert under a full moon. I'm telling you, the desert's one of the most beautiful, peaceful places on earth. Once you learn how to deal with it, it's like the best place you could think of being."

I couldn't help thinking that it sounded a little weird. The interesting thing to me was how Amber acted toward her brother. She just gazed out the window at the dried out brush and rocks. It seemed as if she simply tuned him out—as if she didn't even hear what he was saying. I wondered if maybe she'd gotten into the habit of doing that when her brother talked too much.

As he drove, Luke glanced over at Amber and me. It didn't seem to bother him that Amber was staring out the window. I sort of got the feeling that he was used to her not listening to him, but he saw that I was listening.

"The thing that amazes people is the incredible amount of life that actually exists in such a hostile place," he said. "You've got cacti and yucca and a bunch of other plants. And all kinds of insects and reptiles and animals."

"I guess most of them must live underground during the day," I said.

"Right." Luke nodded. "And who says people can't live that way, too? And they do. I mean, I know people who live underground and they say it's the best."

Just then, Amber turned and gave her brother a funny look, as if she didn't believe him, but Luke either didn't notice or just ignored her.

"You live underground," he continued, "and it's never too hot or too cold. Man, you run some electricity and running water in there, and what else do you need?"

"Windows?" I guessed.

Luke grinned. "Yeah, the views underground

23

aren't so good. But at night, man, you can come out, and then you've got the whole desert to look at."

I just nodded. Frankly, the idea of staring at walls all day and the desert all night didn't sound exactly thrilling.

At least not to me.

7

The road through the desert seemed endless, but at least there were some interesting things to see. Distant reddish ridges and plateaus lined the horizon. Sometimes beyond them, I'd catch a glimpse of a faraway gray silhouette of a mountain.

It seemed as if you could almost see forever. Even dozens of miles past The Last Place on Earth, we could still see the long black plume of smoke rising into the air from the tire fire.

Then I saw a sight that puzzled me.

"What's that?" I asked, pointing at half a dozen tiny black specks circling high in the sky off in the distance.

Luke peered up through the windshield. "Buzzards."

"What're they doing?" I asked.

"Waiting for something to die," Luke answered.

I gave him a puzzled look.

"They're scavengers," he explained. "Eaters of the dead. It's amazing how those things can smell death. You never see 'em, and then out of nowhere they're up there, circling and waiting. I guarantee you, way down on the ground under those buzzards is a coyote or a jackrabbit that's on his way to the big desert in the sky. And as soon as he's gone, they'll be down there, tearing the dead flesh off his bones."

The thought of it made me shiver. When I looked up, I found Luke watching me in the rearview mirror.

"Hey, don't get freaked, dude," he said. "It's the natural cycle of life and death. Old creatures die so that young creatures can live. Something's always going to eat the dead. If it's not the buzzards, then it'll be maggots or worms or microbes. Then someday they in turn get eaten. It's kind of weird, man, but without death there could be no life."

I wasn't certain if what he was saying was true. But I was certain that true or not, thinking about it sure didn't leave me feeling very good.

Meanwhile, Paul hadn't lifted his nose from those pamphlets. He must've finished the one on desert survival, because now he was reading one about the life of the desert. It always annoyed me when he got into reading that way. I guess it was because it wasn't something I could do. I just never found books that interesting. Or maybe it was just that there always seemed to be a lot of other more interesting things to do.

"What's so interesting about that pamphlet?" I asked him.

Paul looked up. "Did you know that most deserts are located near oceans?"

"So?" I said.

"Think about it," he said. "Wouldn't you figure that any place near an ocean would have lots of water?"

"Uh, yeah, I guess you're right," I admitted. "So what's the story?"

"In places where the desert is near the ocean, there's usually a mountain range between them," Paul explained. "Like here, it's the Sierra Nevada mountains. So what happens is, the sun evaporates the water from the ocean and makes clouds. Then the clouds drift inland, but they hit the mountains. And the only way the clouds can get past the mountains is by going up over them. Only the higher you go, the colder it gets, and that makes the clouds condense and then you get rain. So the clouds dump all their rain on the mountains and that leaves nothing for the desert."

27

"Not quite true," Luke said from the front, where he must have been listening in. "It does rain in the desert. I've seen it."

"But not very often, right?" Paul asked.

"More often than you'd think," Luke replied. "Only—the rain never reaches the ground."

"I've heard of that," I said, kind of glad that I could add something to the conversation. "The air's so hot and dry it absorbs the water before it hits the ground."

"Right," Luke said. "So you're standing there and it's thundering and lightning's all around and you can actually see these huge misty sheets of rain coming down. Only it never gets to you."

Amber turned her gaze from the window and looked at her brother. "You've seen that?" she asked, as if, once again, she didn't believe him.

"Uh, yeah, sure," Luke answered.

Amber stared at her brother a moment more, then turned and stared out the window again.

8

It wasn't long before Luke began to slow down the van again. Both Paul and I quickly craned our necks to see why, but all we saw outside was the same old desert. Then, just past a crudely hand-painted sign that said CACTUS FARM, Luke made a right turn off the highway and onto a bumpy dirt-and-rock road into the desert.

"We going to a cactus farm?" I asked.

"Sort of," Luke answered.

"Sort of?" I repeated, puzzled.

"You'll see," Luke said with a mysterious smile.

We continued to bump and bounce down the road for another five minutes. Through the back windows, Paul and I watched the long trail of yellowish dust kicked up by the van.

Finally, the van stopped, and I quickly saw the "cactus farm"—only it wasn't really a farm. It was just a small plot in the middle of the desert sectioned off with a crudely built barbed wire fence. Inside the fence, someone had planted a whole bunch of cactus.

I did have to admit that it was kind of interesting. There were tall, thin ones with arms that reached toward the sky and short, fat ones that looked a little like green pumpkins with red and yellow thorns. Another kind looked like many paddles, one growing out of the other.

Paul, Amber, and I got out of Bertha. Half a dozen small brown lizards scampered out of our way as we walked toward the plants.

"I've seen these before," Paul said, bending over one of the pumpkin-shaped cacti. "Just not this big."

"That's a barrel cactus," Luke said. "People have them in their houses. And these prickly pears, too." He stood next to one of the tall ones with the arms that reached toward the sky. "Here's the one you don't see a lot. The saguaro."

"You see 'em on TV," Paul said.

"Right," said Luke with a smirk. "In the old days, pioneers walked through this stuff. Or they rode through it. They lived in it. Now everything we know about nature comes from watching the tube in our comfortable air-conditioned houses."

30

I was tempted to ask what was so wrong with that, but I had a feeling I'd only be inviting a lecture I didn't want to hear.

Paul put his hands on his head. "It's too hot," he said, and headed back to the van.

The rest of us soon followed. It wasn't long before we'd returned to the highway to continue the trip to Las Vegas.

Or so I thought . . .

"Whoa! Look at that!" Luke suddenly slammed on the brakes. In the passenger seat, Amber jammed her hands against the dashboard to brace herself and keep from being flung forward. In the back, Paul and I tumbled over and wound up in a heap.

The van bumped and lurched off the highway. Once again, we were headed off into the desert to look at something. In the front, Amber stared silently at her brother. I wondered if she was thinking the same thing as me: *How many times are we going to stop and look at something Luke finds interesting?*

We didn't lurch through the desert for long before Luke brought Bertha to a stop and hopped out. This time, Amber, Paul, and I were slower to follow.

"Does he do this a lot?" I asked.

"Sometimes," Amber answered with a shrug.

31

"I know it's kind of strange, but I promise you we'll get to Las Vegas sooner or later."

"Hey!" Luke shouted and waved from outside the van. "Come on! You've gotta see this!"

We all climbed out and went to see what Luke had found. Once again, the sun was almost unbearably hot on our heads. This time it turned out to be the skeleton of some animal. The bones were bleached white from the sun.

"A coyote?" Paul guessed.

Luke shook his head. "Too big for a coyote."

"A wolf?" I guessed, judging from the shape of the head.

"It's a good guess," Luke replied. "Only there aren't any wolves around here."

"Then what?" asked Amber.

"My guess is a dog," Luke said.

I grimaced at the thought. "What would a dog be doing out here?"

"Hard to say," Luke answered. "Maybe he was in a car crossing the desert and he just jumped out and ran away. Maybe he wandered away and got lost. Guess it doesn't matter. The result's the same either way."

The result was an animal that perished in the desert—an animal that didn't belong here. I looked around at the barren sand and rocks and had an uncomfortable feeling.

We didn't belong here, either.

9

Back in Bertha, we bounced across the desert toward the highway. I was glad when we got back on the paved road where we wouldn't get thrown around quite so much. Paul and I had just gotten settled in the back when once again, the van lurched to a stop and we were thrown forward.

Now what?!

I waited for Luke to announce that he'd just noticed some other unique desert feature that he just had to show us. This time, though, Luke turned the van off the highway and started to drive through the desert without a word.

Looking out the back window, I could see that we were now bumping through the desert, parallel to the highway. I crawled up to the front and looked out.

"Where are we going?" I asked.

"There," Luke answered with a nod of his head.

I looked ahead, but I didn't see anything that resembled "there." All I saw was more desert.

"Where?" I asked.

Luke didn't answer. He just drove. I glanced at Amber, but she only shrugged. I stared out the windshield, wondering what was next.

The answer came in the form of some tire tracks that seemed to wind off through the desert toward the hills in the distance. When we reached them, Luke turned the van and started to follow them. I looked back. Through the dusty rear windows I could see the highway receding farther and farther away in the distance.

I turned back to Luke. "Listen, I'm really trying to not be a pain, but I think the rest of us are wondering where we're going this time."

"I'm not sure," Luke answered.

He's not sure, I thought with a deep inward groan.

"How about an educated guess?" Amber asked, forcing a smile on her face.

As the van swerved down the faint tire tracks, Luke bit the corner of his lip. "I'm not positive, but I think the Fort Irwin Artillery Range is at the end of this road."

10

I assumed I hadn't heard him right. An artillery range? No one in his right mind would drive into an artillery range.

Would he?

Maybe the problem was that I was starting to wonder if Luke was in his right mind. Fortunately, Amber must have been thinking the same thing, because she very calmly turned to her brother and asked, "Why would we be going there, Luke?"

"My friend Jake said you could find cool stuff in there," Luke answered.

"What kind of cool stuff?" Paul asked.

"Artillery shells and dud rockets and stuff," Luke answered. "There are things out there that army nuts will pay a ton of money for."

35

"What's an army nut?" Paul asked innocently.

"I think it's someone who collects army stuff," I explained.

"But couldn't we get killed in the process of finding the stuff?" Amber asked. "Like blown up or something?"

"It's doubtful," Luke answered. "I mean, what are the chances that the army's gonna be doing artillery practice this afternoon? Know what I mean?"

"What if they are having practice?" Amber asked.

"We'll hear it and leave fast," Luke said.

It didn't seem as if you could change Luke's mind once he'd decided to do something. No matter what objections we came up with, he always seemed to have an answer.

Meanwhile, Bertha bumped along, following the road—but it wasn't a road. It was just a couple of tire tracks. Through the van's rear window, I watched the highway grow tiny, then eventually disappear from sight.

11

For a while, the artillery range looked like just more desert, a vast expanse of the same old rocks and sand and dried-up brush. Here and there, we passed some cool-looking saguaro cacti, but they weren't anything we hadn't already seen that afternoon.

I was just about to point that out when Luke suddenly slammed on the brakes and jumped out of the van. He was gone before any of us had a chance to ask him what was going on. We watched through the window as he jogged away from the van and into the desert.

I have to admit that at first I thought he'd really flipped his lid, but then I saw something that made me change my mind. A few moments later, despite the heat and brutal sunlight, I was also jogging away from the van and across the desert.

It wasn't long before Amber and Paul followed. Soon we all stood with Luke on the edge of a perfectly round crater in the ground. It was about as wide as a suburban street and maybe four or five feet deep in the center. I had to admit that I'd never seen anything like it.

"An artillery shell made this," Luke said, kneeling down at the edge. He ran his fingers through the loose sand and came up with a small, dark object. "Here, have a look."

He handed me the object. It was hardly larger than a small stone, but it wasn't stone at all. It was metal.

"From the shell," Luke said.

I have to admit that despite my concerns about ever reaching Las Vegas, I was pretty interested. A lot of boys fantasize about army stuff when they're little, and I had been no exception. Even though I'd pretty much grown out of toy guns and plastic army men, finding something like a piece of authentic artillery shell was enough to pull me right back in.

Excited by the find, Paul and I searched through the crater for our own souvenirs. Any concern about our distance from the highway was far, far away.

We both found small pieces of bent metal.

When we got back into the van, our thoughts were mostly on what we were going to do with them.

"I'm gonna put mine on a chain and wear it around my neck," I said.

"I think I'm just gonna mount mine on a piece of wood," said Paul. "Like with a little sign saying it was a piece of an artillery shell."

Luke began driving again. Bertha bounced along, but Paul and I were lost in thought about what we would do with our newfound souvenirs. Maybe I just assumed that we'd head back to the highway now and make a serious effort to reach Las Vegas. It wasn't until Amber looked across at her brother and cleared her throat loudly that I realized I might be wrong.

"When are we going to head back to the highway?" she asked.

I looked out of the window and was surprised by what I saw. We were no longer in the flat desert. All around us were rises and gullies. Something told me we'd headed away from the highway instead of back toward it.

"Where are we?" I asked.

"Along the edge of the foothills," Luke answered.

The shadows from the sun were long, and during those brief moments when we could see the mountains, they were lit by a deep orange light that bordered almost on reddish.

It was getting late—near dark.

"Shouldn't we be heading back toward the highway?" I asked.

"Don't worry about it," Luke said.

"I am worried about it," Amber said. "It's going to be dark in a little while."

"No sweat," answered Luke. "We'll head back fairly soon. Besides, I'm pretty sure there's supposed to be a full moon tonight."

I knew there was no point in arguing. Luke would do whatever he felt like doing, no matter what we said. I was starting to regret that we'd gone on this "adventure." Either we should have taken the bus or we should have told Luke that we really didn't like all the detours.

He was bigger and older than us, though, and we were the guests, so out of politeness, we'd said nothing. Now it was starting to get dark in the back of the van. Paul and I had no choice but to settle in and wait.

12

It grew dark not only inside Bertha but outside as well. Because there was nothing to see, the constant jostling in the back of the van made me start to feel a little carsick. Maybe it was my imagination, but it felt as if the bumping and bouncing were getting worse.

"Are you sure this is the way back to the highway?" Amber asked. She sounded tense and uneasy.

"Pretty sure." Her brother's answer was clipped.

In the back, Paul and I braced ourselves as the lurching continued. Meanwhile, it seemed to be getting darker outside. Amber craned her neck to look up through the windshield.

"I thought there was going to be a full moon," she said uneasily.

"Maybe the moon's just not up yet," Luke speculated.

The words were hardly out of his mouth when the front of the van suddenly dropped as if the ground beneath it had simply disappeared. In the back, Paul and I were thrown forward.

Crash!

13

Everything was quiet. The van was tilted forward at a steep angle, as if it had fallen halfway into a hole. Paul and I were pressed against the front seats. The loudest sounds were our own quick breaths. My elbow throbbed where it had banged into the back of Luke's seat.

"Everybody okay?" I asked.

"I am," said Paul.

"Oh, man, my head!" groaned Luke.

The only one I hadn't heard from was Amber.

"How about you, Amber?" I asked.

"Just shaken up, I think," she answered.

"Guys, there's a flashlight back there somewhere," Luke said. "See if you can find it."

I knew we wouldn't have to look far. Just about everything in the back of Bertha except

43

the mattress had tumbled forward along with Paul and me. After feeling around in the blankets for a moment, I came up with the flashlight and handed it to Luke.

I heard the door on Luke's side of the van creak as he pushed it open. Then the flashlight beam came on. It didn't seem like the strongest beam I'd ever seen. I watched it sweep around the front of the van. Luke must have been surveying the damage.

The rest of us climbed out of Bertha and stood with Luke. The weird thing is that it felt just as hot as it had during the day. It was true that the sun was no longer beating on us, but the almost suffocating heat was still there.

I watched as Luke shined the flashlight on the van. Just as I'd suspected, the front was tipped forward into a small gully. Between the front and rear wheels, the body of the van rested on the edge of the gully. Luke got down with the flashlight and peered under the van. Then he stood back up.

"I'm pretty sure we'll be able to get her out," he said, clicking off the flashlight, "but we're gonna need the car jack and a lot of rocks. We'll have to wait until the morning."

The morning . . .

That meant we were going to spend the night in the desert. But where?

44

14

"Let's get the mattress out," Luke said as he started around the back.

"We can't all fit on it," Amber pointed out.

"We can lay some blankets on the ground, too," Luke said. "Come on, dudes, give me a hand."

I started toward Bertha, but Paul hesitated. "I'm not so sure you want to sleep outside," he said.

I could barely make out Luke's frown in the dark. "Why not?"

"In the summer months like this when it's really hot, most insects and reptiles hide during the day and come out at night," Paul answered.

"How do you know that?" Luke asked.

"I just read about it," my brother said.

"So?" Luke seemed to scoff at the idea. "Big deal. You want to know why most people get bit? Because they bother the animals. If you leave them alone, they'll leave you alone. Now, how about a hand with the mattress."

Paul and I helped Luke get the mattress out of the back of the van and lay it on the ground. We watched as he sat down on it, pulled off his boots, and then pulled a blanket over him. Meanwhile Amber, Paul, and I stood beside the van in the dark.

Lying on his back on the mattress, Luke slipped his hands behind his head and gazed upward. "Hey, what a night. I'm kind of glad the moon isn't out, because you can see the stars. You guys should take a look."

I turned to Paul, but he shook his head.

"What are you gonna do?" I asked.

"I'm staying in the van," he answered.

"But it's all tilted," I said. "You'll never get to sleep."

"Thirty different kinds of scorpions live in this desert," Paul replied. "Plus nearly a dozen kinds of poisonous snakes, black widow and brown spiders, Gila monsters, and centipedes."

"Sure." Luke chuckled. "And I suppose you think they're all right here. It's a big desert, little dude. There might not be a snake for miles."

Paul didn't even answer him. He just pulled

open the back doors of the van and climbed in. He was funny that way. Once he made a decision, he stuck to it, no matter what. Usually his stubbornness drove me crazy, but this time I was kind of glad.

I gave Amber a questioning look.

"I think I'll stay in the van, too," she said. "How about you and your brother stay in the back and I'll stay in the front?"

"Fine with me," I said. I held the door for her while she climbed in.

"You guys'll be back out in no time," Luke called behind us. "There's no way you're going to be able to get comfortable in there."

We got into the van and closed the doors. Luke was right. It was impossible to find a comfortable position on the tilted metal floor. And Amber didn't have it any easier just because she was in the front.

"I can't sit in the seat," Amber groaned in the dark.

"Maybe you should slide down onto the floor and see if that's better," I suggested.

We could hear her moving around on the other side of the seats.

"Well, this is a little better, but not much," she finally said.

Meanwhile, Paul and I weren't having much luck getting comfortable in the back.

"You think maybe we should sleep outside?" I finally asked. "At least we'll be able to lie down flat."

"Not me," Paul answered. "I may not get much sleep in here tonight, but I won't get much sleep out there, either. Not when I'll be thinking about all those desert critters."

"I hate to say it, but I have to agree," said Amber.

No one talked after that. The only sounds inside the van were our sliding and scraping as we tried to find comfortable positions. In the moments when we were still, we heard sounds from outside: the howl of a coyote in the distance, sometimes the sound of something scampering nearby.

I lay awake for a long time, wondering what would happen the next day. We were stuck in the desert. Luke seemed pretty confident that we'd be able to get out of this mess, but I wasn't sure how much confidence I had in Luke.

Mostly, I was starting to think that we really should have taken that bus.

15

"**O**w! Darn it! Darn it all to heck!"

The agonized shouting woke me the next morning. I was surprised that I'd actually fallen asleep. I was pretty sure I'd spent most of the night awake. A few times, I'd dozed for a moment, then woke feeling uncomfortable, twisting around until I found a new position. Feeling stiff and achy, I sat up and looked around. The air in the van was actually cool. All the windows were covered with a film of moisture.

Angry grunts and moans were coming from outside the van.

"What was that?" Paul asked in his groggy morning voice.

"It must be Luke," I answered with a yawn.

Already, Amber was pushing open the front

49

door to see what had happened to her brother. Paul and I scrambled out of the van behind her. Outside, the air felt cool and fresh, just as it had in the van. Luke was sitting up on the mattress, rocking back and forth and groaning. He had one boot on and was holding his other foot, which was bare.

"What happened?" Amber asked.

"Scorpion in my boot," Luke answered through gritted teeth. He pointed at the mattress where a smashed scorpion lay twitching. It was a big pale one.

"Look at the size of that thing!" Luke groaned. "What's gonna happen to me?"

"It's gonna hurt for an hour; then you'll be okay," Paul said.

Both Amber and Luke looked at Paul in amazement. Of course, they didn't know that he'd read the desert survival pamphlet. Once my brother read something, he almost always remembered it.

"How do you know?" Luke asked.

Having been asked this question many times before in many other circumstances, my brother knew that all the explaining in the world wouldn't help. He climbed back into Bertha and got the pamphlet.

" 'The venom of most scorpions is relatively nontoxic to humans,' " he read to them when he came back. " 'Many bites go unreported and are no more harmful than a honeybee sting. Symptoms are generally restricted to the site of the sting. Intense pain normally subsides within one hour, giving way to tenderness and tingling.' "

Luke seemed to calm down a little, but not entirely. He pointed at the smashed scorpion on the mattress. "Maybe most scorpions aren't harmful, but what about that sucker? It's so big."

" 'The only scorpion found in the Southwest that is considered life threatening is the bark scorpion,' " my brother read. " 'It can be distinguished from other less toxic species by its slender pincers, dark coloring, and small size. The mature bark scorpion rarely exceeds an inch and a half.' "

We all stared down at the smashed scorpion. It was light-colored and close to three inches long.

"Does it still hurt?" Amber asked her brother.

Luke nodded. "Yeah, but somehow I feel better knowing it's not gonna kill me."

Wincing, he pulled on his boot and got up. Now that he seemed to be okay, I took a moment to look around. It was growing light out, but the sun was still behind the barren, rocky mountains to the east. Those mountains were the closest to us. As Luke had said the night before, we seemed to be in the foothills leading to them.

Meanwhile, to the west spread a vast desert area filled with gullies and boulders and ravines and low ridges. Farther west beyond that loomed a long line of dull brownish mountains.

Luke limped back to Bertha. Now we could clearly see how it was tipped into the shallow gully. Amber's brother opened the back of the van and pulled out the kind of jack you normally used to fix a flat tire.

"Here's the deal, dudes," he said, limping around to the front of the van. "We've got to jack up the front and get rocks under the tires. We'll build a path of rocks under each tire so that we can back right out of the gully. So start collecting rocks."

"Like what size?" I asked.

"They should be pretty big," Luke said. "Like at least the size of a plate. And it'll help if they're sort of flat."

Paul, Amber, and I started to look around. There were plenty of rocks around us, but not a lot of them were the size of plates, or flat.

"I guess we'd better spread out," Amber said.

"Just be careful," Paul warned us.

"He's right," I said. "Before you pick up a rock, turn it over with a stick and make sure there's nothing under it."

16

We each found a sturdy stick and then spread out to look for rocks. At first it wasn't such bad work. We'd find a rock and carry it back to the van. Using the car jack, Luke would lift the front end and we'd slide the rocks under the front tires. Meanwhile Luke used some of the other rocks to start to build tracks up out of the gully.

The sun rose quickly, and with it came a heat that reminded me of the day before when we'd stood close to the fire. Soon my forehead was damp with sweat and the sun beat down on the top of my head, making it feel hot and tight. At first when I'd turned over stones, there'd been some moisture darkening the underside, but now the stones were as dry on the bottoms as they were on the tops.

The next time I returned to Bertha, Luke had stripped off his shirt. His tanned shoulders glistened with sweat as he worked in the sun.

"How about something to drink?" I asked.

"I was just thinking that myself." Still limping slightly, Luke started around to the back of the van and pulled the water can off the back door. You could see by how he struggled with the big can that it must've been really heavy. Then he got a tin cup from inside Bertha. He opened the top of the water can and tilted it slightly. Delicious-looking fresh water spilled out. Luke handed me the cup. The water was warm, but it was still refreshing. A moment later, Paul and Amber joined us.

"Great idea," said Amber, who gladly accepted a cup of water and gulped it down.

Paul went next.

"Am I the only one who's hungry?" Paul asked after his water.

"I'm starved," I said, and Amber nodded in agreement.

"Let's see what we've got." Luke went into the van again. Out came a small box of Special-K cereal, some stale bread, and a bag of dried fruit. Not the most appetizing brunch, but we must have been really hungry because ten minutes later we'd eaten every crumb.

"It is really getting hot," Amber said. "Maybe I should cut these jeans down to shorts."

"I wouldn't," Paul warned her.

"Why not?" asked Amber.

"I bet that's what it says in that survival pamphlet, right?" Luke said, then chuckled.

Paul nodded. "It says you should wear long sleeves and a hat."

"Well, I'm not saying you're wrong," Luke said, "but I figure we're gonna be back on the road in another hour and it's not gonna matter either way. So if my sister wants to cut her jeans into shorts, I say she should go ahead."

We all looked at Amber. Her eyes darted from Luke to Paul and back.

"On second thought," Amber said. "These jeans are practically new, so maybe I won't cut them."

I don't know why I didn't think of my baseball cap sooner, but now Paul and I put ours on. Amber didn't have any kind of a hat.

"Maybe you could take a shirt and wear it like a scarf on your head or something," I suggested.

But Amber shook her head. "I'll look like a jerk."

We kept looking for rocks. The first few had been easy to find and pretty close by, but we needed a lot and soon we were walking hundreds of yards to find them and bring them back. Meanwhile, the sun pounded down on us. It almost felt as if its rays were a heavy force, like weight pushing us down. Finally, I had to rest. Even with my hat, I had a headache from the sun and felt as if the heat had drained every bit of energy out of my body.

"I've got to get out of the sun," I said after walking what seemed like a mile to find a rock.

"Can't blame you," Luke replied, looking pretty drained himself.

"The only problem is—how?" said Amber. She was right. The sun was directly overhead. There was no escaping it.

We decided to drag the mattress back into the van and get inside. It was hot inside. We couldn't keep the doors open because that made the interior lights go on and Luke was afraid that would drain the battery, so we had to stay in Bertha with the doors closed and the windows open. At least it was out of the sun.

The front seats were scalding, so Amber and Luke sat with Paul and me on the mattress in the back. We started out sitting with our backs against the van's walls, but it wasn't long before we'd each curled up on a corner of the mattress. The sleepless night before, combined with the draining heat, had left us all ready to take a nap.

17

It was late afternoon when I woke up. The others were still curled up on the mattress asleep. Through the windows I could see that the sun was more than halfway down in the afternoon sky, but it was still incredibly hot.

For a while I just lay there, wondering what would happen next. Luke's plan sounded like a good one. I just hoped that once we got the van out of the gully, we'd head straight to Las Vegas without any more detours.

It wasn't long before the others woke.

"This isn't so bad," Luke said with a yawn as he rubbed his eyes. "All we did was take a siesta. It's what people in hot climates have been doing since the beginning of history. It's already starting to feel cooler. We'll get the rest of the rocks and be out of here by night-fall."

It sounded good, but like a lot of things that sound good, it was easier said than done. As long as the sun was anywhere in the sky, it was still hot; and we had to walk farther and farther to find the rocks. The farther we went, the longer it took to bring them back and the heavier they felt.

I had just dropped a rock off and was headed out to find another one when I saw Paul in the distance. He appeared to be standing perfectly still and staring down at something on the desert floor. I didn't think much of it and turned away to find a suitable rock.

It wasn't long before I found a rock and started back toward Bertha. The rock was about the same size as the others I'd found, but either it was heavier than the others or I was just tired, because I soon found that I had to put it down and rest.

I had just put it down when I noticed that Paul was standing in the same place I'd seen him before. That seemed odd. It had been at least five minutes since I'd last seen him. Why hadn't he moved?

I decided it was worth investigating and went to see. Paul was facing me, but he didn't see me because he was staring at the ground.

I couldn't imagine what he'd found that was so interesting. As I got closer, I could see something on the ground, maybe two feet from him. At first I thought it was some kind of light brown funny-shaped rock.

But as I got closer, it became clear that it wasn't a rock at all.

And then I heard the high-pitched rattling sound.

18

The rattler was curled up in striking position. I'd actually never seen that before. The only snakes I'd seen were in the zoo, and they either didn't move or just looked bored—but this snake was anything but bored. Its tail stood straight and rattled just the way snake rattles always sound on TV and in the movies. Its head was raised and its mouth was open, revealing its deadly venom-filled fangs.

It couldn't have been more than two feet from Paul's leg—easily close enough to spring forward and bite him.

I stopped about 15 feet away. Paul looked up at me with a terrified expression on his face.

"Don't move," I whispered.

Paul's lips became crooked. "Duh," he whispered back.

In the quiet desert afternoon, the rattling sound filled the emptiness. Although I didn't know for sure, I had the feeling that this situation wasn't like the one with the scorpion that had bitten Luke. It was my understanding that rattlers were deadly. This wasn't like a bee sting. This was a slow and agonizing death with no way to get help.

"What should I do?" Paul whispered.

A few possibilities skipped through my mind. What if he sprang backward, out of the rattler's reach?

Maybe that would work—or maybe the rattler was so fast that it would bite him anyway.

Or maybe I could jump up and down and stomp on the ground to draw the rattler's attention away from my brother.

Or maybe that would just make the snake more tense and likely to strike at my brother.

"What did the pamphlet say?" I asked.

Paul blinked at me. It almost seemed that in his fright he'd forgotten to think of that himself.

"You're supposed to relax and not move," Paul whispered. "They say snakes are like dogs. They can smell fear."

"So go ahead and relax," I whispered.

"Yeah, right." Paul smirked, but it did seem to me that he loosened up a little. For a nine-

61

year-old, sometimes my brother really amazed me.

I don't know how long we stood there, but for once I was hardly aware of the sun. Finally, the snake stopped rattling and closed its mouth.

Then it lowered his head and uncoiled.

The snake slithered away.

My brother's shoulders sagged with relief and he actually sank down to the sand as if his legs had gone weak.

I went over and put my hand on his shoulder. "You okay?"

"Yeah." He nodded and slowly rose up. "Thanks for staying with me, Henry."

"Hey, piece of cake." I grinned to hide my huge relief.

We picked up our rocks and headed back toward the van. The sun had turned red and was just a little bit above the mountains in the west now. When we turned and looked at the mountains and plateaus to the east, they were bathed in a reddish gold light. It would have been a beautiful sight, if only we weren't trapped in the desert.

"You know, only about a dozen people actually die from snakebites each year," Paul said as we walked, "even though more than seven thousand are bitten."

"How can that be?" I asked.

"The venom doesn't act that fast," my brother said. "Most people have time to get help."

It took me a second, then I realized what he was saying. "But you couldn't have gotten help out here."

"Yeah," Paul said with a nod. "I know."

We walked a little way without talking and then Paul said, "So what do you think?"

"I think . . . next time we take the bus," I answered.

"I meant about these rocks," Paul said.

"I know that's what you meant," I said. "I was just trying to make a joke. I don't know what to think about these rocks. I just hope it works."

"You really think Luke knows what he's doing?" Paul asked.

"I sure hope he does," I answered.

Now the van was in view.

But something didn't look right.

The hood was up, and half of Luke's body seemed to disappear into it, as if he were being eaten.

As Paul and I got closer, we could see that Luke was working on Bertha's engine. Amber was sitting on a pile of rocks near him, with her chin in her hands. Luke had placed a couple of greasy, blackened engine parts on rocks so that they wouldn't get filled with sand.

Paul and I put down our rocks. Luke straightened up and backed away from the hood. His forearms and hands were smeared with black grease.

"Where've you dudes been?" he asked, wiping the sweat from his forehead and leaving a dark streak of grease instead.

"Paul ran into an unfriendly rattlesnake," I answered.

Amber looked up, startled, but Luke just nodded. I was sort of surprised that he didn't bother to ask if my brother was okay. I guess he had other things on his mind.

"What's going on with the van?" Paul asked.

"She won't start," Luke answered.

19

Paul and I stared at each other, and then at Luke.

"I tried to start her a few minutes ago and she just wouldn't catch," Luke explained.

Bertha wouldn't start. That meant that even if we did get it out of the gully, we still wouldn't be able to get out of the desert.

"Has this ever happened before?" I asked.

Luke nodded. "Look, she's a pretty old vehicle. Things go wrong."

"What do we do?" Paul asked.

"We fix it," Luke answered. "I figure a wire got jarred loose when we went into the gully last night, or maybe some sand got into the carburetor. Whatever it is, it shouldn't take long to fix."

"Should we keep looking for rocks?" Paul asked.

Luke put his hands on his hips and looked around. "Naw, little dude, it looks like we probably have enough."

"Can we just rest for a while?" Amber asked. "I'm totally drained."

"Sure, go ahead," her brother replied.

We crawled into the back of the van again. It wasn't rocks we needed now. What we needed now was patience to wait until Luke fixed whatever was broken.

By now the sun had dropped behind the mountains in the west. It was becoming twilight. According to Luke's plan, we should have been just pulling Bertha out of the gully and heading across the desert, but outside, the light was disappearing, and engine parts were still scattered everywhere. Unless Luke started to put them back very soon and very fast, we would be spending our second night in the desert.

We sat in the back and waited. My stomach growled angrily with hunger, but there was nothing I could do about it. Drinking water helped fight the thirst, but not the hunger. Again, even in the shade inside the van, even in the twilight, it was sweltering. You had the feeling that it must have taken all night for the desert to cool off. Then, maybe in the final hour before dawn, it would grow comfortable—just in time for the sun to come up and start baking everything again.

It was getting dark when Luke came around to the back of the van. His skin glistened with sweat. His arms below the elbow were blackened with grease and he had streaks on his forehead where he must have absentmindedly wiped the sweat away. Strands of long blond hair fell into his face, and the tops of his shorts were stained dark where the sweat from his body had soaked in.

"Looks like we're gonna be here for another night," he announced.

So tell me something I don't *know!* I thought.

We watched as Luke tipped the water can over to pour some water into the tin cup we'd all been sharing. Was it my imagination, or did he have to tip it way over before any water came out? A scary thought struck.

"You think maybe we should ration the water?" I asked.

"A common misconception," Luke announced as if he'd been waiting for someone to fall into a trap. "All the experts say you should drink as much as you need."

I glanced at Paul and he nodded. "That's what the survival pamphlet says, too."

"But it looks like we're running low," I said.

"Don't worry," Luke said. "I'll have this thing back together in the morning and we'll be on our way. We'll stop at the next place and get all the water we need."

Now that we'd jacked up the front of the van and put rocks under the front wheels, it was almost level. There was no way Luke was going to sleep outside again. In the back, we each staked out a corner of the mattress and curled up. Exhausted from the heat and work of gathering the rocks, we quickly fell asleep.

20

When I woke the next morning, the sun was already up and the air inside Bertha felt warm. Soft clanks and clunks came from the front of the van, meaning that Luke was back at work on Bertha's engine. I looked around. Paul was still curled up in sleep, but Amber was awake. Her face was bright red and looked swollen. I was confused for a moment, then remembered that she'd been out collecting rocks without a hat all the previous day.

"Are you okay?" I asked.

"My face feels like it's burning," she answered.

"I think you got too much sun," I said. Talk about an understatement!

She nodded. "I guess I'd better stay in the shade."

I sat up. The mixed sensations of thirst and hunger seemed to come into focus at exactly the same moment. It was hard to say which one was worse. They were both pretty bad.

The tops of my ears and the back of my neck throbbed painfully. I had a feeling that because my baseball cap didn't cover those parts of my head, they were pretty badly burned, too.

The only comforting thing I could think of was what Luke had said the night before—that it wouldn't take him long to put Bertha back together and get us going.

More clanks and clunks came from the front of the van, but from the back, I couldn't see what it meant. I could only imagine that Luke was putting it all back together.

Curious to see if I was right, I climbed out of the back of the van and went to look. It was already hot out. This was our second day in the desert and my whole body felt dry, dusty, and gritty. The thought of jumping in Dad's nice cool swimming pool almost brought tears to my eyes.

Just as I'd hoped, the greasy motor parts were no longer scattered on rocks around Bertha. That meant Luke must've put them back into the van. I found Luke under the hood, bent over the engine. He was concentrating so hard on what he was doing that he didn't even notice me at first. I was struck by the grim, determined look on his face. This wasn't the same happy-go-lucky, not-a-care-in-the-world Luke with whom we'd started the trip. The lines on his grease-blackened face were deep with worry.

It took a few moments before he saw me. He nodded and grunted a hello, then turned back to the engine.

"So how's it going?" I asked.

"Not bad," Luke replied without looking up. "I figure another half an hour and then we'll start her up and get out of this godforsaken place."

The way he said it led me to believe that his big romance with the beauty and majesty of the desert had ended. Now he wanted to get out of there just as badly as we did.

"Anything I can do to help?" I asked.

"Drink of water would be nice," he answered.

I went around to the back of the van where the water can was and started to tip it over toward the metal cup we all shared. I tipped it farther and farther over until it was almost on its side. Finally some water sloshed out.

I brought the cup back to Luke and handed it to him.

"There's not much left," I said.

Luke nodded as he sipped the water from the cup. "As soon as we're out of here, we'll refill it."

If we get out of here, I couldn't help thinking.

With nothing to do except wait, I climbed into the back of the van again. Paul was up now. His face was streaked with dirt and his eyes were bloodshot.

"How's it going?" he asked.

"Half an hour," I answered, crossing the fingers on both hands.

And so we waited. The sun was getting higher and the inside of the van was starting to feel like an oven again. It was hard—no, impossible—to imagine how desert nomads lived like this, facing the unrelenting heat day after day.

Finally the front door squeaked and Luke jumped into the driver's seat.

"Okay, girls and boys!" he cried gleefully as he slid the key into the ignition. "Let's get ready to rumble!"

He turned the key.

I have to admit that I held my breath.

The engine turned over and made that whiny, sluggish sound all engines make when they need a little while to start.

Guh . . . guh . . . gruuummmmmmm! The engine sputtered and caught!

"Yahoo!" Luke yelled, then twisted around in his seat so he could look out behind as he backed the van over the rocks and out of the gully. In the back, we all shared happy, relieved looks.

72

Whatever doubts we'd had were gone. We were going to get out of this mess.

"Swimming pool, here we come!" Paul said with a grin.

Luke put the van in gear. We felt Bertha back up a few inches.

Suddenly the motor made a loud blubbering sound and a huge cloud of white smoke burst out of the tailpipe. The smoke seeped into the back and smelled like burning oil.

The engine went dead.

The van started to roll back into the gully.

Luke quickly jammed on the brake.

Bertha stopped rolling.

In the back, we sat in silence, watching the big cloud of white smoke slowly rise and disperse into the sky.

In the front, Luke turned the key.

The engine cranked over and over.

But it wouldn't start.

21

I don't know how long we sat there in silence after that. I felt hopeless, stunned. We weren't getting out of the desert after all.

So now what?

Sitting in the back with us, Amber pressed her hands to her face and started to sob. I caught Paul's eye. He was sitting with his knees pulled tightly under his chin, looking miserable and scared.

Meanwhile, Luke twisted around in the front seat and glared at his sister. With the grease all over his arms and smeared on his face, he looked like some kind of wild man.

"Stop it!" he shouted at her. "Crying doesn't help anything!"

Amber stopped for a split second, probably out of surprise. Then she started sobbing again.

I felt uncomfortable. Why was he yelling at her? She wasn't doing it on purpose.

Luke whirled back around in his seat and slammed his hands angrily against the steering wheel. "Stupid girl," he muttered.

"It's not her fault," Paul said.

I don't know who was more surprised—Luke or me. We both stared at my brother in disbelief. I expected Luke to say something, maybe even yell at Paul, but instead he slid out of the front seat and slammed the door closed with a bang.

In the back of the van, Paul and I sat with Amber while she cried. I could understand how she felt. I was pretty scared, too. I wished I could put my arm around her or something, but I was worried that it might not be the right thing to do.

After a while, she wiped her eyes on the sleeve of her shirt.

"I'm sorry," she said with a sniff. "I'm just scared."

Paul and I nodded.

"We're scared, too," I said.

"What are we going to do?" Amber asked.

I couldn't think of a good answer. Angry muttering and clanking were coming from the front of the van. It sounded like Luke was going back to work on the engine.

"You think he knows what he's doing?" Paul asked.

We both looked to Amber for the answer.

"I don't know," Amber said. "I mean, I've seen him work on the engine a million times, like on the street outside our house, but I never really paid attention to what he was doing."

"What if he can't get it fixed?" Paul asked.

It was a good question.

Then I had an idea. "We were supposed to get to Las Vegas two nights ago. Wouldn't they be out looking for us?"

Amber, Paul, and I shared uncertain looks.

Amber bit her lip and shrugged. "I sure hope so."

"Maybe they've already started looking for us and they just can't find us," Paul said.

"But what can we do?" Amber asked.

The memory of that long column of smoke rising from the fire behind The Last Place on Earth came to my mind.

"I've got it!" I said. "We'll build a fire!"

22

"Hey, go ahead," was Luke's response when we told him our idea. "I just don't know what you're gonna find around here to burn. Creosote, I guess."

Small, gnarly creosote bushes were spread out all over the desert. They accounted for most of the gray-green dots we saw. After telling Amber to stay in the van because of her sunburn, Paul and I went out and tried to gather some for a fire.

"Gee, what's with these things?" Paul groaned as he held one by the branches and tried to pull it out of the earth. The plant wouldn't budge.

"Too many roots," I guessed.

Fortunately, Luke hadn't bothered to take out some of his smaller gardening tools when he'd unloaded Bertha back in Pasadena. Under some garden hose I found a pair of pruning shears, but even with them it was hard to cut through the branches of the tough little plants.

With a lot of sweat and effort, we managed to gather a small pile of creosote branches and other odd sticks.

"What do we light it with?" Paul asked.

I looked back at Bertha. "Gasoline."

Luke hesitated when we asked him for gasoline. "All I've got is whatever's in the tank," he said.

"We won't use much," Paul said. "We can siphon a little out."

Luke frowned. "Look, I know you want to help and everything, but why don't you just chill out in the van until I get this fixed, okay?"

Paul and I glanced at each other out of the corners of our eyes, as if daring each other to ask what would happen if he "fixed" Bertha again and it still didn't start.

Finally, Paul spoke up. "We just figure it can't hurt to start a fire."

Luke let out a sigh. "Okay, we'll siphon off a little gas and see what happens."

Using the garden hose, we siphoned a small amount of gas into a plastic pop bottle. Luke found an old pack of matches in the glove compartment and wished us luck.

Back at the pile of branches and sticks, I poured the gasoline and lit it. The pile burst into flames. A small cloud of smoke rose into the air, then quickly thinned out and disappeared.

It took only a few minutes for the pile to burn itself down into a heap of grayish embers. Paul and I stared at it in disappointment. There'd hardly been any smoke at all.

"What do we do now?" Paul asked.

"Go back to the van," I said.

With the burning hot sun beating down on us, we walked back to Bertha. I had a feeling Luke had seen everything we'd done, but he didn't say anything. He just kept working on the motor.

Paul and I climbed into the back again. It felt like an oven, but at least it was out of the sun.

"I watched from the window," Amber said as we tipped the water can over. "I guess it was worth a try."

Paul and I each had a couple of cups of water. It wasn't enough, but I was afraid to take any more.

Paul pulled his legs up under his chin again. "What do we do next?" he asked.

"We can't stay here," I said. "We're almost out of water. We have to go."

"But we don't know where," Amber pointed out.

"Then we have to figure out where," I said.

"How?" Paul asked.

"By going to the highest place around here and taking a look," I said.

"We can't climb during the day," Amber said. "It's too hot."

"Then we'll go at night," I said.

"That's better anyway," said Paul. "At night, we'll be able to see lights. Then we'll know which way to go."

It was decided. We would wait until that night, climb the closest hill, and figure out which way to go.

But first we had to get through the rest of the day.

It wasn't long before Luke came around to the back of the van to pour himself some water. I watched the expression on his face as he tipped the water can farther and farther over. When the water finally sloshed out, he poured himself only half a cup.

"I guess we'd better start conserving water," he said.

This time there was no talk about its being a common misconception.

"How much?" Paul asked.

"I don't know," Luke answered. "How about a cup a person every two hours?"

"That's a quart per person every eight hours," said my math wizard brother. "Three quarts a day per person times four people is three gallons."

Luke picked up the water can and sloshed it around, as if trying to guess how much water was left. I knew what a gallon of milk weighed. You could tell from how easily Luke picked up the can that there was probably a lot less than three gallons inside.

"A cup every three hours?" Luke asked.

"Two quarts a day," Paul said.

Luke shook his head in frustration. "That's about half of what a person in the desert is supposed to have."

"Actually," said Paul, "according to the pamphlet, if people stay in the shade, don't move much, and breathe through their nose, they can survive on less."

"Breathe through your nose?" Luke replied with a skeptical snort. "Fine, you three can do that if you want, but I have to keep working on the van."

"It's not like we have a lot of choice," I said.

Luke nodded in agreement, then poured out the other half cup he was entitled to. He brought it to his lips and drank it down. Then he stared into the empty cup. "If that's all for the next three hours, this ain't gonna be easy."

23

The rest of the day passed slowly and with growing discomfort. Luke kept working on the van. The rest of us stayed in the back. Even in the shade, it was stifling hot. We dozed and woke, our mouths and throats parched. Paul's suggestion about breathing through our noses was a good one—it kept our mouths from drying out. But every time I dozed, I must've started breathing through my mouth again, because I would wake up and hardly be able to swallow.

As night began to fall, the parts Luke had once again taken from the engine were still scattered on rocks around Bertha. It was obvious that Luke would not be able to put them all back before dark. Amber, Paul, and I huddled in the back of Bertha and discussed our plan.

"What if he doesn't want to do it?" Paul whispered.

"We'll tell him he has to," I said.

Amber shook her head. "That won't work. Telling my brother he has to do anything just guarantees that he won't do it."

"Then what do you suggest?" I asked her.

"We have to tell him that this is what we've decided to do and we're going to do it whether he likes it or not," Amber said.

Paul raised an eyebrow. "And what if he still refuses?"

"Then we'll just have to do it without him," Amber said.

Paul and I shared a look. I wondered if Amber knew how nervous both of us were about going anywhere in the desert at night by ourselves.

"Suppose we don't go," I said. "Suppose we stay and just pray that he gets the van to work?"

"There isn't enough water left," Paul said. "If he doesn't get the van to work tomorrow, we're sunk."

"Unless we climb up tonight, figure out which way to go, and do it," Amber said.

The sun continued to drop. It wasn't long before Luke came around to the back of the van.

"How's it going?" Amber asked.

Her brother let out a sigh and shook his head.

"It's too soon to tell. I'll just have to start working again in the morning. Then we'll see."

"By then we'll be out of water," his sister said.

"Yeah, but if I can get Bertha going—" Luke began.

"What if you can't?" Amber asked. "Are you just going to let us all die out here?"

Luke narrowed his eyes at his sister. "No one's gonna die. I'll get her to work. I don't see what other choice we have."

The rest of us shared a knowing look.

"Wait a minute," Luke said. "What have you guys been talking about while I've been working?"

"We think we should climb up the hill and try to look around," Amber said. "If we can see some lights, we can start walking in that direction."

"You mean a town?" Luke asked.

"I mean anything," Amber said. "If we see car lights, we'll know there's a road. We can go that way and flag down a car. It's better than staying here."

"I told you I'll get Bertha going," Luke stressed.

"That's what you said yesterday," Amber snapped.

"Yeah, but . . ." Luke began but didn't finish. He bowed his head and ran his greasy fingers through his hair. "Okay, but what if you don't make it before the sun comes up?"

"What if we stay here and the van doesn't start?" Amber asked back.

Luke let out a long, slow sigh.

"We might not have to climb very far," Paul said hopefully.

"Lights can be deceiving," Luke said. "They can be a lot farther away than you think."

"I guess we'll just have to look for the brightest ones and hope they're the closest," I said.

"Yeah," Luke agreed with a smirk. "Sure."

24

There didn't seem to be much point in waiting. The sunlight was almost completely gone. The sooner we went out, the better. We started up the gully Bertha had gotten stuck in. Pretty soon we were in a ravine between two slopes. We started to climb one. It wasn't easy. We were tired, parched, and hungry. Even though the sun was going down, the heat rising from the earth was unrelenting. We'd put our hands on a rock and it would feel hot—sometimes too hot to touch.

Climbing up through the rocks and brush was easier than climbing through the sandy spots on the slope, where we had to climb on all fours, using our hands as well as our feet. The sand was hot and it got into our shoes and socks and rubbed painfully against our skin. For every two steps up, we'd slide back one, all the while breathing in hot air and the dust we kicked up as we climbed.

We were halfway across one stretch of sand when Luke stopped and straightened up. His feet disappeared in sand up to his ankles.

"What's the point of this?" he asked, looking around in the dark. "I can't see a thing."

Just the slightest sliver of moon had appeared off to the west. It wasn't nearly enough to provide any light that might help us see where we were going.

"We have to go up higher," I said.

"It's stupid," Luke argued. "Even if we get to the top of this hill, we're still surrounded by mountains. You can't see anything."

"I don't remember passing any mountains on the way here from the highway," Amber said. "If we can just figure out where the highway is, we can head in that direction."

"We could easily be twenty or thirty miles from the highway," Luke said.

"I bet we could walk twenty miles tonight if we had to," I said. In school I'd learned that people walk at a rate of around three miles an hour.

"You'd be lucky to get two miles in this terrain," Luke said.

"Wait a minute, guys," Amber interrupted. "It's silly to stand here and argue. We're almost out of water, and without it we'll die. We have to do something."

As if trying to set an example, she clawed her way up the sandy slope, passing her brother in the dark.

"I'm with her," Paul said and started to climb, although at a slower pace.

I looked at Luke. Without a word, he shrugged and started to climb.

A little while later, I reached the top of the slope. I could just barely make out the shape of my brother, standing among some rocks, his hands on his hips.

"See anything?" I asked.

"No," Paul answered.

"Guess we'll have to climb higher," I said.

"We've got a problem, Henry," my brother said somberly.

"What's that?" I asked.

"I can't find Amber."

25

He was right. There was no sign of her among the rocks and sparse brush.

"Maybe she climbed higher," I said.

Paul twisted around and looked upward. From where we were standing, we could see up the face of the hill. Even without much moonlight, there was enough starlight to see that nothing above us was moving.

Luke made it to the top of the slope and joined us.

"We can't find Amber," I said.

He frowned and looked around, then cupped his hands around his mouth and shouted, "Amber!"

Her name echoed back faintly from the hills around us.

"Amber!" he called again.

Paul and I joined him. "Amber!" We'd shout, then wait for an answer, then shout again.

It didn't take long for it to become clear that she wasn't going to call back.

Luke muttered a curse under his breath. "Great. Now what?"

"We have to find her," I said.

"I've got news for you, dude," Luke said angrily. "People don't just disappear off hillsides."

"Maybe she fell and banged her head," Paul suggested.

"You want to spread out and look for her?" I asked.

Luke didn't answer. Just ahead of us were some large rocks. Luke climbed up to them and looked around.

"Over here!" he suddenly called.

Paul and I scrambled up through the rocks and joined him. On the other side of one of the rocks was a dark open hole in the ground. It wasn't huge, but it was definitely large enough for someone Amber's size to fall into.

Luke got down on his knees and cupped his hands again. "Amber?" he shouted down into the hole.

"Luke? I'm hurt." We all heard her voice.

It sounded weak and far away.

90

"Do you think you can climb out?" Luke called down.

"I'm stuck," she called back. "I can't get out. It's dark. I'm scared."

"Okay, don't worry—we're going to come get you," Luke shouted. "Do you have any idea how far down you are?"

"I fell," Amber called back. "I don't know how far. Not far, I guess, but I'm stuck. It's dark. Please hurry."

"Don't worry," Luke called again. "We're going to stay right here and get you out."

In the dark, Luke looked into our faces. "Any ideas?" he whispered so his sister wouldn't hear.

"What about the hose?" Paul asked.

Luke shook his head. "It won't be long enough."

"Then we'll have to make it longer," I said.

"How?" Luke asked.

"Wait here," I said and turned to Paul. "Come on, let's go."

My brother and I hurried down the hill. It was easier to get down that steep sandy slope than it was to climb up it, but once we hit the rocky slope below, it was slower going. Not every rock was firmly planted in the ground. If we stepped on one that was loose, we could easily fall and twist an ankle, or worse.

We picked our way down through the rocks and brush in the dark.

"Ow!" I heard Paul grunt in pain behind me.

"You okay?" I stopped.

"Yeah, just bumped into a sharp edge," he answered.

"Be careful!" I urged him.

"No, I'll really try to smash into something next time," he answered sarcastically.

We made it down to the van. I started to reach for the door. Suddenly I heard a loud, threatening snarl come from inside.

26

Something large jumped out of the driver's side window. Whatever it was shot past me and dashed away into the dark. It must have been a coyote, looking for food. It was a strange, scary feeling—as if the desert had come alive and was pushing in on us from all sides, never giving us a moment to breathe.

"What's wrong?" Paul asked when he caught up to me and found me standing beside the van, shaking.

"Nothing . . . I think," I answered. "There was something in the van—a coyote, I guess—and it kind of freaked me."

Paul looked around in the dark. "You think anything else is in there?"

I tried to peer through the open window into the van. "Don't know."

"You know, it's not just coyotes," my brother said. "All the cold-blooded things come out at night. The insects, reptiles, spiders—"

I cut him short. "I know that. You don't have to remind me. Come on. We'd better get that hose."

We both knew that one of us had to climb into the van to look for the hose, but neither of us moved. Who knew what critters had gotten in there while we were climbing the hill?

"Well, what are you waiting for?" I said, hoping Paul would go first.

"Why don't you go?" he asked.

"Look," I said impatiently. "This is no time to chicken out. We have to help Amber."

"Right," said Paul. "So you go in there."

There was no point in arguing. Paul had to be as scared as I was. I reached for the door handle, yanked open the door, then jumped back, waiting to see if anything came out.

When nothing leaped or crawled out, I crawled in. I found the hose we'd used to siphon the gas, but Luke was right. It didn't seem long enough.

"We're gonna have to cut the straps off our backpacks and tie them together," I told Paul.

In the dim interior light of Bertha, Paul and

I got to work. It quickly became obvious that the straps alone wouldn't make the hose long enough either.

"It's still not enough," I said. "With all these knots, it's hardly longer than the hose was to begin with."

"Then let's use our clothes," Paul suggested.

"Good idea," I said.

We dug into our packs and started tying long-sleeved shirts and jeans together. The shirts worked the best, but we didn't have many of them. Next, we tied on the blankets by their corners.

Finally, we had something. It didn't look like much, but as long as it held together, it might just be long enough to help get Amber out.

I looped the clothes and hose over my shoulder. "Let's go."

"Wait." Paul went around to the front of the van and rolled up the windows.

"Good idea," I said, and we started back up the hill.

27

Once again, we had to climb through the heat rising out of the earth. My throat was so dry I could no longer swallow. My eyeballs felt gritty, and no matter how many times I blinked, I couldn't make the feeling go away. My whole body felt tired and weak. The only thing that kept me going was the knowledge that Amber was in trouble.

By the time we got to the beginning of the sandy slope, my legs were aching. They felt as if they were going to cramp up at any time.

I paused and looked back at Paul, who was struggling up through the rocks behind me. Our eyes met in the dark. I guess because we were brothers and had spent our whole lives together, we didn't even have to speak to know what each of us was thinking.

"We have to do it," I said.

Paul nodded grimly. I felt a surge of pride inside. For a slightly pudgy kid who spent most of his time playing computer games and reading books, he was turning out to be pretty gutsy.

We started up the sandy slope.

Two steps forward . . .

One slide back . . .

I was so tired, I had to climb with my hands on my knees, almost lifting each leg with my hand and setting it down. The muscles in my thighs jerked and spasmed.

"Henry? Paul?" Luke's voice called down from above.

"We're coming!" The sound of my voice caught me by surprise. It was like the croak of an old man who'd smoked cigarettes his whole life.

We were coming, but each step was growing harder and harder. I could feel my heart pounding and my temples throbbing. With my feet buried in the sand over my ankles, I bent over and rested with my hands on my knees.

"Come on!" Luke urged us from above.

"I'm coming as fast as I can," I gasped, then lifted my right foot out of the sand and took another step. It would have been nice if I could have handed the hose off to Paul for the rest of the way, but he was a dozen yards below me, having his own problems climbing up.

Finally, I made it up to the rocks where Luke was crouched over the dark hole in the ground.

"Here you go." I handed him the clothes hose.

Luke looked it over and tugged at a few of the knots. "Good. Great. Good work."

He leaned back toward the hole. "Amber?"

"Yes?" Her voice sounded weak and distant.

"I'm going to send down a line," Luke said. "Yell when it gets to you." Luke started to feed the clothes hose into the hole, but it wasn't long before he stopped.

"What's wrong?" I asked.

"It's not going down," he said. "It's bunching somewhere before it gets to Amber."

"Maybe we could tie a rock to the end of it," I suggested.

Luke shook his head. "It's not like it's a smooth drop. It's steep enough to fall down, but still on a slant. There must be bumps and snags the clothes are catching on."

"So what can you do?" I asked.

Luke stared at me in the dark for a moment. "Someone's going to have to go down and bring the line to her."

28

Luke's words were still echoing in my ears when Paul reached us.

"What's going on?" he asked.

"The line won't go down by itself," I answered. "Someone's going to have to crawl down there and bring it to Amber."

In the night, I watched Paul stare at the hole in the earth. "Down there?" He swallowed.

There was no way in the world he was going to do it. He was a brave little kid, but he was still only nine. The problem with Luke was just the opposite. He was simply too big to fit. That meant there was only one person left who could do it: me.

Luke leveled his gaze at me. "I'd go down there in a second if I could fit."

As if I didn't feel bad enough about the situation we were in already, now a heavy, doomed feeling came over me like a shadow.

"Luke?" Amber's nervous anxious voice echoed up from below.

"Yeah, sis?" Luke called back.

"What's happening?" she asked.

"Don't worry," Luke called down to her. "We're just getting ready to come get you."

"Hurry. I'm scared. It's really icky down here."

Luke looked back at me. "Ready?"

I was overcome with nervousness. "What do you think it is, anyway? An animal's cave?"

Luke shook his head. "Just an old miner's excavation. The hills are filled with them. They'd dig in a ways and poke around. If they didn't find anything promising, they'd move on. I bet this hole doesn't go more than twelve or fifteen feet down." He held the hose end of the line toward me. "Tie it around your waist, okay?"

I slid the hose around my waist and knotted it. Now there was nothing left to do except go. A big part of me wanted to hurry up and help Amber—we couldn't get out of the desert until I did—but another part of me was scared. Who wouldn't be?

I got down on my hands and knees and peered into the hole. It was absolutely pitch dark. Crawling down in there would be like disappearing off the face of the earth. I reached in with my hands and felt the walls of the hole. They were partly dried, crumbly dirt and partly smooth rock. The hole went down on a steep slant, but not a straight drop. I backed up and looked at Luke.

"You're gonna have to hold onto the line so I don't lose my grip and fall on Amber," I warned him.

"You got it." Luke took hold of the line.

I turned and looked at Paul. He gave me a thumbs-up.

Here went nothing. I ducked into the hole and started to crawl. It was hard to get a grip. My hands either slid over the lose soil or over the slippery, dusty rock. The opening was just wide enough for me to be able to slide down. Luke was right. There was no way he would have been able to fit.

The path downward twisted and turned as it passed between and around the underground boulders. The hose was tight around my waist, but though it rubbed uncomfortably, I was glad it was there. Without it, I would have slid help-lessly to the bottom.

"Who's that?" Amber's voice sounded close.

"Henry," I answered as I slid closer.

"You're knocking dirt on me," she said.

"I don't mean to," I said. "Keep your eyes closed."

I was going down head first, reaching around blindly every inch of the way. Now I could hear Amber breathing.

"You okay?" I asked.

"I can't tell," she answered. "I think so, but I'm stuck. It hurts."

I crawled down a little farther and felt something.

"You're touching my leg," Amber said.

I felt around a little more and reached her other leg, then her hand. She must've fallen backward down the hole and now she was wedged, back first, at the bottom with her arms and legs sticking up. No wonder she couldn't get free.

"What's it feel like?" I asked.

"Like I'm caught between two rocks," she answered.

I could picture the miner digging down to this point between the rocks, then realizing he couldn't go any further and giving up.

"Okay, I'm going to try to pull you free," I said. "I'll try not to hurt you."

I took hold of one of her ankles and one of her hands and tried to pull, but it was no use. I couldn't get a grip. All I managed to do was spill more dirt onto her.

102

"Stop!" Amber cried. I could tell she was scared that she'd be buried.

I let go and twisted my head around, trying to face out of the hole.

"Luke!" I yelled.

"Yeah?"

"You have to pull on the line!" I yelled. "Not too hard. Just steadily. I'll tell you when to pull harder."

"Gotcha!" Luke called back.

"Okay," I said to Amber, taking her ankle and hand again. "We're going to try it this way. When I start to pull, you try to shimmy out if you can."

"I'll try," Amber answered.

Gripping her ankle and hand as tight as I could, I yelled up to Luke, "Pull!"

The hose around my waist tightened and I began to inch backward. I could feel Amber's grip tighten as I began to back away.

"Ow!" Amber cried as I lost my hold on her hand.

"Stop pulling!" I yelled up to Luke. "Give me a little slack."

Once again, I reached down to Amber. She was crying now. I could hear her sniff and sob.

"It's not going to work," she whimpered.

"It has to," I said. "We have to try again. Give me both of your hands."

She reached up and I grabbed her hands. They were slippery. Even though it was pitch black in the hole, I could imagine our hands, sweaty and covered with a thin film of slippery dust mud.

"Henry?" Amber's voice came out of the dark.

"Yes?"

"Sorry. I just got really scared for a moment."

"That's understandable."

"Thanks for coming down here to get me."

"No sweat." I twisted my head around and yelled up to Luke. "Pull slowly!"

The hose tightened painfully around my waist, rubbing hard against my skin. I pulled on Amber's arms as she tired to wiggle free.

"Come on!" I grunted, trying to wedge myself against the cave walls and pulling as hard as I could.

Suddenly I felt something give—but it wasn't Amber. It was part of the cave wall crumbling, pouring an avalanche of dirt down around us!

29

Then next thing I knew, the air was filled with dirt and dust. I could feel a layer of dirt on my head and arms. I was coughing like crazy.

"Henry! Amber! Answer me!" The sound of Luke's panicked shouts were in my ears, but I couldn't answer. All I could do was cough.

In between my coughs, I could hear other coughs. It must've been Amber. That was good news. At least she wasn't buried.

"Henry! Amber!" Luke shouted from above.

I tried to answer: "We're . . ." *Cough!* "Okay . . ." *Cough!* "I think."

"Amber too?" Luke called down.

I reached down and felt for her hands.

"Can you breathe?" I asked.

Between coughs, Amber managed to grunt, "Yes . . . but I'm . . . covered . . . with dirt."

"Grab my wrists this time," I said, reaching down.

As soon as our fingers touched, we slid our hands around each other's wrists. Amber squeezed tight. I had a feeling she wouldn't be letting go this time.

"Luke!" I shouted. "Pull!"

The hose went tight again. Amber and I kept hold of each other's wrists. She was squeezing so tight it felt as if she was cutting off the circulation to my hands. More dirt and small stones fell down around us, but we held on, knowing this was our last chance.

Tighter . . .

Tighter . . .

With a sudden lurch, I felt her pull free. Still holding on with one hand, I used the other and my feet to brace myself as I pulled her up and out.

Now that she was free, Amber could hold onto my arms and climb. We slowly made our way up. At times it felt as if she was going to pull my shoulder right out of its socket, but as long as we were getting out of that hole, I almost didn't care.

All at once I felt hands around my ankles. Luke must've grabbed them. He pulled me out, then grabbed his sister and got her out.

I just lay next to the hole, gasping for air. At least the air outside wasn't filled with dust.

"You okay?" Paul asked me and Luke asked Amber at the same time.

"Yeah," I answered.

Amber was in Luke's arms. She coughed and nodded, but at least she was out of that hole.

For a long time I just lay there looking up at the starlit sky. I couldn't remember ever being as glad to get out of a place as I was to get out of that hole. The hot desert air felt great compared with the stuffy, dusty air I'd been breathing in that death trap.

It turned out that Amber was okay. She must've been pretty banged up and bruised from that fall, but she could walk. As we headed back down the hill, Luke walked beside me.

"Thanks for helping Amber," he said.

"It's okay," I said.

"You could've been buried down there," he said.

"It's a good thing I didn't know that *before* I went down there," I replied.

It was hard to tell what time it was when we got back to Bertha. All I knew was that it was the middle of the night and I was so sore and exhausted that all I wanted to do was put my head down and sleep. Everyone else must've felt the same way, because without a word, we all crawled onto the mattress in the back.

Whatever plans we had for escape would have to wait until the morning.

30

The next time I opened my eyes, I was curled up on the mattress and sunlight was pouring in through Bertha's windows. It was incredibly hot in the van, but what else was new?

I looked around at the other three bodies curled up on the mattress. Everyone was covered from head to foot with a film of reddish brown dirt. Everyone's hair was tangled and gritty, their lips swollen and cracked.

I heard someone moan. It was Amber. She was curled up in a ball and still asleep. Even though we were all pretty badly sunburned by now, she somehow looked pale and ill. Still sleeping, she moaned again.

My eyes left her and drifted over to Paul. His eyes were open and he was looking back at me.

"What's wrong?" he whispered.

"I don't know," I whispered back.

Paul pointed at a spot on Amber's arm. It resembled a bull's-eye with a dark reddish center surrounded by a ring of pale white skin. Outside the ring, the skin was red and inflamed like a bad sunburn.

"What is it?" I whispered.

"Don't know," he whispered back.

"Maybe it's in a pamphlet," I said.

Paul turned around and opened one of the pamphlets. Amber groaned in her sleep again. Luke snored a little, then snorted and changed position. My mouth was so dry it felt like it had a layer of dust inside it. I reached over to the water can. There was hardly any water left now. I poured out a cup and took a sip. I didn't even have a chance to swallow the water. It just seemed to disappear the moment it touched my tongue.

I took another sip and felt some water trickle down my throat. Then I passed the rest of the cup to Paul, who looked up from his pamphlet and took it gladly.

"Is there much left?" he asked, holding the empty cup out toward me.

"A few cups, if we're lucky," I answered. It wasn't easy to talk. My throat felt tight and sore.

Paul lowered the cup in disappointment. He had to be thinking what I was thinking: *We're stuck this time. Really stuck!*

And time was running out.

The sands of time, I thought ruefully.

Paul turned back to the pamphlet. I lay on my side, a demanding growl in my stomach reminding me that I was starving and parched. Every pore on my body felt clogged with grime. The heat was sapping every ounce of my strength.

My thoughts drifted aimlessly. In school, we'd read about how they used to burn witches at the stake in the old days. I'd always thought that being burned alive would have to be about the worst form of death imaginable, but now I began to wonder. At least with burning, you'd die pretty fast. Maybe being slow-cooked to death was even worse.

"Listen to this," Paul said in a hoarse voice. " 'The fiddleback spider of the Southwest is sometimes mistakenly referred to as the brown recluse, which resides in the Midwest. At first, the bite of this spider results in little or no pain; however, the bite will eventually evolve into a bull's-eye lesion with a dark center outlined by white and set on a red and inflamed background.' "

I looked again at the mark on Amber's arm. Paul's description fit it almost exactly.

"Is it bad?" I asked.

" 'Flulike symptoms and nausea,' " Paul read.

I felt bad for Amber, but did it matter? Would anything matter by the end of this day?

Luke stirred and stretched, then slowly sat up. "Oh, man!" He groaned and pressed his fingers against his forehead as if he had a throbbing headache. It seemed to take him a while to focus on the rest of us.

"What's going on?" he asked.

"We think Amber got bitten by a spider," I answered.

Luke wrinkled his grease- and dirt-smeared forehead. "Why?"

I pointed at the mark on her arm. "Paul read about it in the pamphlet."

Luke blinked. His eyes looked sunken in his head. "We have to get out of here." He started to heave himself up toward the driver's seat.

"We can't," I reminded him. "The van's stuck. There are pieces of the engine all over the place."

Luke looked puzzled. "I need some water."

I poured some in the cup and handed it to him. He quickly drank it and held out the cup. "More."

"I think we'd better save the rest," I said. "There's hardly any left."

"What do you mean?" Luke asked. "The can was full."

"We've been drinking from it for the past two days," I explained.

"It was full yesterday," Luke insisted. "What'd you do with the water?"

Paul and I shared a nervous look. Luke wasn't making sense.

Luke started to get up again. "I'd better see what's going on." He seemed to have trouble getting in between the front seats and out the van's door. Outside, he stumbled, then regained his balance. Paul and I watched through the window as he staggered around in the sun, picking up parts of the engine and then dropping them in the sand.

"What's wrong with him?" I whispered to Paul.

"He lost more water than the rest of us," Paul whispered back. "All that time he spent working in the sun with his shirt off."

"We better get him back in the van," I said.

Paul and I got out. The sun was like torture. Luke was just standing there. Suddenly, I noticed something weird: shadows fluttering over the sand.

I looked up.

High in the sky above us circled half a dozen buzzards.

31

They're scavengers ... I could recall Luke's words clearly. *Eaters of the dead. It's amazing how those things can smell death. You never see 'em, and then out of nowhere they're up there, waiting. I guarantee you, way down on the ground under those buzzards is a coyote or a jackrabbit that's on his way to the big desert in the sky. And as soon as he's gone, they'll be down there, tearing the dead flesh off his bones.*

Despite the heat all around us, I felt a shiver of fear and looked over at Paul. He was looking upward, too.

Luke was still wandering around. I went over to him.

"We'd better get you back in the van," I said. "This sun'll kill you."

Luke shook his head. "We gotta go."

"There's nowhere to go," I said.

As if he hadn't heard me, Luke started to walk away.

Paul and I watched him. I don't think either of us knew what to do, but the answer quickly came. Luke lost his balance again and sat down hard on the sand.

Paul and I hurried over to him.

"We have to get you back in the van," I said. "Really, Luke."

This time he seemed to understand. He let us help him up. With his arms over our shoulders, we managed to walk him back to Bertha. The sun was brutal and I was starting to get a bad headache, too.

Inside the van, Paul crawled to the water can and tipped it over. Enough water to fill half the cup dribbled out.

"That's it," he said, handing the cup to me.

I wanted to drink that water so bad. I felt as if I would have given everything I owned for it, but I knew it had to be for Luke. He needed it more than any of us.

I held the cup up to Luke's blistered lips. Even though he was half out of things, he knew it was water and gulped it down.

"Now what?" I asked Paul.

Paul rested his chin on his hands and

thought. We were in desperate shape, out of water, dying of thirst. Luke was out of it. Amber was sick from a spider bite. It seemed to me that only a miracle could save us.

Paul raised his head and blinked—he'd just had an idea.

"We have to start a fire," he said.

"We tried that, remember?" I said.

"This time we'll burn the tires," Paul said.

I stared at him for a moment. My first reaction was to say he was crazy. Burning the van's tires only ensured that we'd never get out of there, but I quickly understood what he was thinking. We were way past the point of getting anywhere in Bertha anyway.

"How'll we get them to burn?" I asked.

"The garden hose," Paul answered. "We'll siphon some gas."

"Right."

I knew that meant going back into the sun, but now it was a race against time and dehydration. Outside, we managed to jack up the rear end of the van just high enough to get the rear tires off the ground.

Next, it was time to get the lug nuts off Bertha's wheels. The lug nuts looked rusty. I fit the tire iron over one of them and tried to turn it.

It wouldn't budge.

"I can't get it!" I grimaced, throwing all my weight against the tire iron.

Paul grabbed it and pulled, too. Together, we gave it all we had.

Splang! The tire iron slipped off the lug nut. Paul and I went flying backward and landed on the hot sand.

"It's useless," I gasped, lying in the scalding sun. "We'll never get the tires off."

Paul lay near me, breathing hard. From his silence, I knew he was thinking. But there had to come a point where even he ran out of ideas, and I had a feeling he'd reached that point.

He rose to his hands and knees on the sand. I'd never seen him look so dirty and haggard. "Henry?"

"Yeah?"

"There is a way," he said.

"How?" I asked.

"We . . . burn the whole van."

32

Maybe we were lucky Luke was out of it. Even though it was probably our last chance, I couldn't see how he'd ever agree to let us burn Bertha.

The first thing Paul and I did was get the mattress out of the van. We dragged it far away and propped it up, using rocks and sticks. Then we moved Luke and Amber under it so they would still be in shade. Amber could hardly walk. She was doubled over with stomach pains. Paul and I practically had to carry her.

We turned back to the van. The sun was burning down on us. My head was pounding and I felt nauseated. Above, the buzzards were still circling.

"How do we do it?" I asked as we trudged back to Bertha.

"Siphon gas to the inside?" Paul guessed.

"I saw a show once where they stuck a rag down the gas tank and lit it," I said.

"We could do both," said Paul.

We siphoned some gas out of the tank and splashed it around the inside of the van. In that heat, most of it evaporated almost instantly. The fumes just added to my headache and nausea.

"Forget it," I gasped. "Let's try the rag in the gas tank."

Paul pulled a T-shirt out of his backpack and stuffed it into the gas tank. He patted his pants pockets.

"Where're the matches?"

The matches? I realized I must've been half out of it myself. I had the matches. I pulled them out of my pocket and staggered over to the van.

I opened the book and tried to tear one of the matches out, but it seemed as if my hands wouldn't do what I wanted them to. My fingers were stiff, the skin cracked.

"Let me try." Paul reached for the matches.

"No, I can do it," I said, and tried again, but I still couldn't get a match out.

119

"You're wiped, Henry," Paul said. "Let me."

I guess we were both pretty focused on the matches, because neither of us saw Luke.

"What are you doing?" he asked.

Paul and I looked up. Luke was looming over us.

33

"Burn Bertha?" Luke asked, slurring his words. "Are you nuts?"

"It's our only chance," I said. Paul had backed behind me in fear.

Luke scowled. "To do what?"

"To make a fire so that someone'll find us," I said.

"Forget it." Luke held out his hand. "Give me those matches."

"No," I said, holding my hands behind me.

"You want to get hurt?" Luke growled.

"I want to get saved," I replied. Behind my back, I held the pack of matches between my fingers and waved them back and forth, hoping Paul would notice.

Luke took a step closer. "I said give me those matches."

Behind my back, I waved the matches like crazy.

Come on, Paul, take them!

"No one's burning my van, get it?" Luke growled. His outstretched hand curled into a fist.

I didn't know what to do. Paul hadn't seen the matches.

"We have to," I insisted.

Luke took another step and reached for my arms.

Suddenly I felt the pack of matches get yanked out of my hand!

I dodged Luke and started to run.

"Come back here!" Just as I hoped, Luke started to follow me.

I was able to run a couple of dozen steps before the heat, my pounding headache, and my cramped stomach forced me to drop to my knees.

Gasping for breath, Luke lumbered up behind me.

"Gotcha!" he grumbled.

Ka-boom!

34

The van was engulfed in flames. A ball of thick black smoke was rising into the sky.

"Bertha!" Luke dropped to his knees on the sand with a stricken, astonished look on his face.

I'd never seen a car burn before, except in movies. Within the crackling flames, I could hear all sorts of small pops and bangs as things exploded. Billowing gray-black smoke rose into the sky.

"I don't believe it," Luke muttered in despair.

I felt bad for him, but I did believe it. That giant smoke signal we'd just sent up in the air was our last hope.

Our . . . ?

Where was Paul?

35

"Paul!" I screamed. It was the adrenaline from pure terror that got me up off the sand and sent me staggering back toward the burning van.

"Paul!" Where was he?

I pictured him on fire, running hysterically through the desert with flames dancing on his back.

Had I seen that, or just imagined it? My heat-addled brain was so dazed I wasn't sure.

"Paul!" I screamed again. I was close enough now to feel the heat from the van. Each time something popped or exploded inside, I'd wince. Where was my brother?

"Paul!"

"Over here."

I turned. Twenty feet away, Paul was lying on his back in the gully. His baseball cap was gone and his hair was standing on end as if he'd just received a big electrical shock. I lurched toward him.

"You okay?" I asked.

"I think so," he said, "considering the fact that I just got blown up."

I helped him up.

"What's going on?" Amber was staggering toward us with wide eyes as she took in the burning van and her brother on his knees in the sand.

"We're sending smoke signals," I said.

Amber scowled, but said nothing.

"Come on," I said, leading her back to the mattress. "You better get out of the sun."

We helped Amber into the shade and then went back and got Luke. He kept muttering about Bertha, but the fight had gone out of him.

I don't know how long we huddled under the propped-up mattress, trying to stay out of the sun. I just lay there, curled up, my stomach cramping and my head throbbing. I think maybe I even gave up a little. Everything hurt so bad, I just wanted it to end.

But then, some sense told me to look out from

under the mattress. Far in the distance, something was moving toward us, kicking up a trail
of dull yellow dust. It was still far away, but
every so often the sun would reflect off it in the
split-second kind of glare you sometimes saw
coming from a windshield.

36

The closest hospital was in Barstow. Paul and I shared a room. We both had IVs. The nurses kept kidding us about how they'd never seen so much liquid go into people and so little come out. They even nicknamed us the "sponge brothers."

It turned out that burning Bertha was what saved us. People saw the smoke 20 miles away in a town called Baker and radioed to the search-and-rescue teams that had been out looking for us for two days.

Dad and Mom both showed up at the hospital. They took turns lecturing us. Mom's lecture was about how incredibly dumb we were to try to save her money and how the next time we'd better take the bus. Dad's lecture was about how incredibly dumb we were to try to blow up the van and how next time . . . well, he just made us both swear there wouldn't be a next time.

But I sensed they were both very happy and even a little bit proud that we'd managed to survive.

The doctors kept us in the hospital for two days. Mom had to go back to Pasadena, but Dad hung around and checked us out of the hospital. We were just going through the lobby when we saw Amber and Luke. They both looked amazingly healthy. Although my sunburn had peeled, Amber's had turned into a tan.

"Sorry we never made it to Las Vegas," Amber said with a sheepish smile.

"Are you kidding?" I said to her, then turned to Luke. "Sorry we burned up Bertha."

"Yeah," Paul agreed. "We just didn't know what else to do."

"It's cool, dudes," Luke replied. "I feel like Bertha sacrificed herself to save us. It was a noble way to go."

Paul and I shared a look. A lot of things had changed, but Luke was definitely still Luke.

Since Luke and Amber were going back to Pasadena while Paul and I would head to Las Vegas with our dad, we said good-bye.

A little while later, we were in Dad's car, on the road to Las Vegas.

"I don't know if you guys are interested in this after all you've been through," Dad said about 20 miles past Baker, "but there's a real interesting place called Cima Dome just off the road a little ways from here. If you wanted to stop and take a look, I'd—"

Paul and I looked at each other with wide eyes. Leave the highway again? "No way!" we shouted.

Then we both sat back and enjoyed the air-conditioning.

ABOUT THE AUTHOR

Todd Strasser has written many award-winning novels for young and teenage readers. Among his best known books are those in the *Help! I'm Trapped in* . . . series. Todd speaks frequently at schools about the craft of writing and conducts writing workshops for young people. He and his wife, children, and Labrador retriever live in a suburb of New York. Todd and his family enjoy boating, hiking, and mountain climbing. You can find out more about Todd at www.Todd Strasser.com.

Todd Strasser's
AGAINST THE ODDS™

Shark Bite
The sailboat is sinking, and Ian just saw the
biggest shark of his life.

Grizzly Attack
They're trapped in the Alaskan wilderness
with no way out.

Buzzard's Feast
Danger in the desert!

Gator Prey
They know the gators are coming for
them...it's only a matter of time.

A MINSTREL® BOOK
Published by Pocket Books

2023

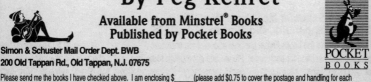

BILL WALLACE

Award-winning author Bill Wallace brings you fun-filled stories of animals full of humor and exciting adventures.

What would you do
if you saw an alien...
in the mirror?

mindwarp ™

For Ethan Rogers, Ashley Rose and Jack Raynes of Metier, Wisconsin, turning thirteen means much more than becoming a teenager. It means discovering they have amazing alien powers. Ethan is a skilled fighter—the ultimate warrior. Ashley can stay under water as long as she wants. Jack can speak and understand any language—human and otherwise.

They don't know why it happened, but someone does...and that someone or something wants them dead.

MINDWARP #1: ALIEN TERROR
MINDWARP #2: ALIEN BLOOD
MINDWARP #3: ALIEN SCREAM
MINDWARP #4: SECOND SIGHT
MINDWARP #5: SHAPE-SHIFTER
MINDWARP #6: MINDWARP
MINDWARP #7: FLASH FORWARD
MINDWARP #8: FACE THE FEAR
MINDWARP #9: OUT OF TIME
MINDWARP #10: MELTDOWN

By Chris Archer

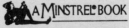 A MINSTREL® BOOK

Published by Pocket Books

1429-05